R0085545606

01/2018

D1432177

The Magic School Bus Rides Again

Sink or Swim

by
Judy Katschke

BRANCHES™

SCHOLASTIC INC.

Ms. Frizzle's Class

Jyoti

Arnold

Ralphie

Wanda

Keesha

Dorothy Ann

Carlos

Tim

TABLE OF CONTENTS

© 2018 Scholastic Inc.
Based on the television series *The Magic School Bus: Rides Again*.
© 2017 MSB Productions, Inc.
Based on the *Magic School Bus*® series © Joanna Cole and Bruce Degen.
All rights reserved.

Published by Scholastic Inc., *Publishers since 1920*.
SCHOLASTIC, THE MAGIC SCHOOL BUS, BRANCHES, and logos are trademarks and/or registered trademarks of Scholastic Inc. All rights reserved.

The publisher does not have any control over and does not assume any responsibility for author or third-party websites or their content.

No part of this publication may be reproduced, stored in a retrieval system, or transmitted in any form or by any means, electronic, mechanical, photocopying, recording, or otherwise, without written permission of the publisher. For information regarding permission, write to Scholastic Inc., Attention: Permissions Department, 557 Broadway, New York, NY 10012.

This book is a work of fiction. Names, characters, places, and incidents are either the product of the author's imagination or are used fictitiously, and any resemblance to actual persons, living or dead, business establishments, events, or locales is entirely coincidental.

Library of Congress Cataloging-in-Publication Data available

ISBN 978-1-338-23214-1 (hardcover) / ISBN 978-1-338-19445-6 (paperback)

10 9 8 7 6 5 4 3 2 1   18 19 20 21 22
Printed in China   38

First edition, January 2018
Edited by Marisa Polansky
Book design by Jessica Meltzer

CHAPTER 1

SNOW DAY, SNOW WAY!

It was a snowy day at Walkerville Elementary. That meant snowball fights!

"Incoming!" screamed Jyoti. Snowball after snowball spit out from her **state-of-the-art** snowball machine.

"You got me!" Ralphie cried as he fell toward the snow.

Arnold huddled by the door. He counted, "Nine hundred hours, six minutes, and . . . six seconds until spring."

For the other seven kids in Ms. Frizzle's class, a snowy schoolyard was a flurry of fun. But for Arnold it meant chattering teeth, cold, wet socks—and his usual countdown to spring.

He kept counting. "Nine hundred hours . . ."

Arnold was so busy with his countdown that he didn't notice a tiny green lizard crawling up to the Walkerville Elementary  roof. It was Liz, the classroom lizard.

"Five seconds," Arnold sighed.

Liz flopped on her belly and slid across the roof, knocking a pile of snow onto Arnold. He looked like a human snowman. "GLUUUUUUH!!" Arnold groaned.

Just then, the bell rang. Arnold's friends headed inside to their classroom. He followed behind them, moving like a frozen robot.

"What's with you, Arnold?" Wanda asked.

"Avalanche," Arnold said through chattering teeth, "in under—derpants!"

"You don't like winter. Do you, Arnold?" Wanda asked.

"I rate it somewhere in between blue cheese and papercuts!" he said.

"Oh, Arn," Wanda said. "You should just do what Ms. Frizzle says. 'Take the rest of it and make the best of it!' Just like I'm going to make the best of today's field trip."

Ms. Fiona Frizzle was full of sayings and surprises. Her biggest surprises were her field trips on her magic school bus. She had taken her students inside a volcano and to outer space! But today's field trip would be a little different.

"I can't believe Ms. Frizzle is letting us pick where we go!" Keesha said excitedly.

"She says we earned it for that time we almost got eaten," said Carlos.

"Which time?" they all said together.

"Anyway, I already have a bunch of ideas for where we could go," Wanda said. She pulled a huge scrapbook from her bag and—THUMP! She placed it on a desk.

"Uh-oh." Ralphie groaned. "Is that your Giant Book of Stuff That Needs Saving?"

"Not stuff, Ralphie," Wanda said, "Species!"

"Species. It means a group of closely related animals," said Dorothy Ann. She was an excellent researcher and liked to share facts and information with the rest of the class.

Wanda flipped to a page and announced, "Here's a great idea. Let's go to the frozen Arctic and save the Aleutian shield fern!"

Aleutian shield fern

Keesha wrinkled her brow. "What's a shield fern?" she asked.

"Arctic?" Arnold cried. "That sounds cold."

"Seriously, Wanda?" Ralphie said. "*We* get to pick where we go, and you want to go somewhere cold?"

8

"It's sweet of you to want to help these creatures," Keesha said, "but how about we save ourselves . . . from freezing? I'm thinking—"

"Hawaii!" a voice called out.

The kids whirled around to see—

"Ms. Frizzle!" everyone shouted.

Ms. Frizzle hula danced into the classroom. Liz strummed a lizard-sized **ukulele** as the teacher threw colorful flower necklaces called leis around her students' necks and said, "Not that I'd ever want to influence your decision, kids. But what if, just this once, our field trip was more of a tropical vacation?"

The kids went wild. A warm weather vacation was exactly what they all needed. Well, all of them except Wanda.

"What about the poor fern?" Wanda asked, holding up a picture.

But nobody heard Wanda. Her classmates were already busy talking about surfing waves and drinking coconut smoothies.

Well, even if we are going on a tropical vacation, I'm going to save something, thought Wanda. *I just have to figure out what!*

CHAPTER 2

MOTION TO OCEAN

Sunglasses and sunscreen, everyone," Ms. Frizzle told the kids as she boarded the bus. "That goes for you, too, bus!"

Ms. Frizzle's magic school bus was very special. The bus could transform into anything Ms. Frizzle needed. It had a Mesmerglober, a Shrinkerscope, the latest information technology, and even a pair of cool new shades.

Ms. Frizzle's students hopped aboard the bus. For once, they were ready for this field trip.

"Bus!" Ms. Frizzle called out, "do your stuff!"

The bus whirled and twirled until it was in the middle of the Pacific Ocean, on the island of Nihoa.

POOF!

"Remember, class," Ms. Frizzle said. "You're still in school, so we need to work on the three R's: resting, relaxation, and riding the waves!"

The students ran toward the ocean. Jyoti rode the waves on her propeller-powered boogie board. Dorothy Ann rested on her raft, and Arnold swam in the ocean with a pair of puffy water wings.

Wanda snorkeled in the shallows and looked for underwater species. A tiny blue-and-yellow striped fish was splashing around.

"What a cute little fish," Wanda said. *But what is she doing all by herself?* she wondered.

Wanda stood up and pressed a button on the side of her mask to talk to Dorothy Ann. She always had all the answers.

"Hey, Dorothy Ann," Wanda said. "There's a tiny blue-and-yellow striped fish near me. I'm going to send you a picture. Can you tell me what kind of fish it is?"

Wanda dunked below the water and pressed the button again. It sent an image of the fish to Dorothy Ann's tablet.

"Common name is bluestripe snapper of the **family** Lutjanidae and the **genus** Lutjanus." Dorothy Ann reported.

"Thanks, Dorothy Ann," Wanda said. Then she dunked back underwater and the fish darted straight through her legs!

"You're cute, bluestripe snapper," Wanda said to the fish. "I'm going to call you Becca Blue!"

Becca playfully poked at Wanda's toes. "Hey, that tickles!" Wanda giggled. "How can such a tiny little fish survive in such a big ocean?"

Her question was answered with a splash. Ms. Frizzle popped up out of the water. "That's a deep question, Wanda," she said. "When you think on it, what bubbles up?"

"Hmm," Wanda said. "Maybe there's nothing dangerous around to hurt her, so—"

"Shaaaaaaaaaaaark!" Carlos shouted.

Did he say shark? I guess there are some dangerous things around! thought Wanda.

"Scratch that!" Wanda said, swimming fast toward the shore. She turned and called, "Be right back, Becca!" Wanda had decided what she was going to save—Becca!

CHAPTER 3
IN IT TO FIN IT

Wanda and Ms. Frizzle ran out of the ocean toward the shore. Carlos and the others stood on the beach. They were all staring at Dorothy Ann's tablet.

"Carlos? Did you see a shark?" Wanda asked.

"Yeah, I saw it on the tablet," said Carlos.

"Check it out, Wanda," said Keesha, pointing to the tablet. "They have so many cool animals on this island."

"Like sharks!" Carlos said.

"I heard," said Wanda, who was still out of breath from running out of the ocean.

"Oooh! What an awesome creature!" Ms. Frizzle exclaimed. "I'd love to meet him!"

"Can we go find the shark?" Carlos asked excitedly. "I'll go with you."

"Me too!" Wanda said. "I need to see what is out there with Becca."

The others stared at Wanda. Becca who?

"Come on, everybody," Ms. Frizzle called back. "Let's find this shark the way the locals do."

"Do you mean the people that live here?" Dorothy Ann asked as they boarded the bus.

"Not the people," Ms. Frizzle said. "You know. The locals . . . down in the ocean! Bus, do your stuff!"

The bus shifted shape into a submarine, then—SPLASH!

Ms. Frizzle sat at the controls as the bus dove into the ocean.

She checked out the buttons on the control panel. There were tons of buttons—like a giraffe button, a dinosaur button, and a fish button. Ms. Frizzle pressed the fish button. Goldfish crackers poured onto her head!

"Oops! Wrong button!" she called out. She tried a different one and—

The students popped out of the bus, each in their own tiny submarines shaped like fish.

"Look at my fishmobile go!" Carlos shouted, doing loops.

"How do you steer this thing?" asked Arnold.

"As my big sister always says," Ms. Frizzle called through the bus's microphone, "take chances. Make mistakes—"

"And get messy!" the kids added.

"Take chances? I guess that means permission to push buttons!" Wanda said with a smile.

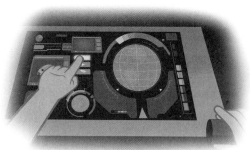

She tried a button.

"Dorsal fin **activated**," an electronic voice reported.

Suddenly, a dorsal fin sprouted from the top of her fishmobile. It helped steady her submarine.

"Guys," Wanda said into her microphone. "Use the dorsal fin to keep from rolling over."

DORSAL FIN

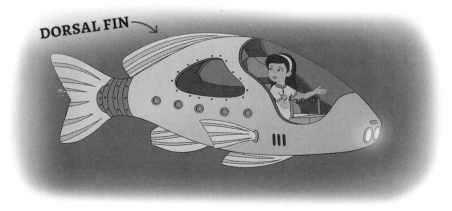

"My tummy thanks you, Wanda," said Tim, steadying his fishmobile.

Ralphie pushed a button.

"Tail fin activated," the electronic voice said.

Ralphie zoomed forward with the help of a new fin at the back of his fishmobile.

"Hey, everybody," Ralphie said into his mic. "The tail fin moves you forward—fast!"

TAIL FIN

"Maybe a little too fast," he said. He headed straight for Dorothy Ann! She quickly pushed a different button.

"Pectoral fins activated," the electronic voice reported as fins shot out the front sides of Dorothy Ann's fishmobile.

"Use pectoral fins for steering," she told her classmates.

PECTORAL FIN

PECTORAL FIN

Ms. Frizzle smiled. "Wow, it looks like things are going swimmingly!"

"WOO-HOO!" Jyoti cheered. "I can swim like a fish!"

"Or like a mermaid!" Keesha piped in.

"This is amazing. I can move just like Becca! Wait up, Becca!" Wanda called to the little fish in the distance.

She was just about to power forward when Ralphie gulped. "Um . . . guys? Look!"

An enormous, scary, dark blob headed right toward them.

"What is that thing?" Keesha asked. "A giant squid?"

"A killer whale?" Carlos guessed.

"Whatever it is," Wanda said, "it's coming straight for us!"

"AAAAAAAAH!" everyone shouted as the strange blob moved closer and closer.

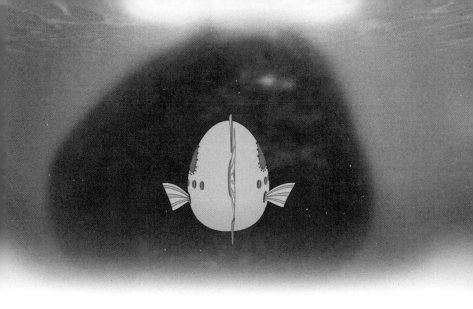

CHAPTER 4
SOMETHING FISHY

Everybody ruuuuuuun—I mean SWIM!"
Ralphie shouted, as he spun his fishmobile
around.

The students pressed buttons as fast as they
could to try to get out of the dark blob's path.

But one student in Ms. Frizzle's class wasn't
going anywhere.

"Listen up, huge, evil, scary thing," Wanda said, staring the creature down through her windshield. "There is no way you're getting between me and Becca!"

The blob was closing in on Wanda! She shut her eyes and held her breath.

When she opened her eyes, the dark blob had changed shape! Wanda was safe—and she was now inside a huge tunnel that went right through the middle of the blob!

It turned out the big blob wasn't a giant squid or a killer whale. It wasn't even big!

Wanda opened her eyes. "No way! The blob was just a whole bunch of—"

"Fish!" yelled the others.

"Not a bunch of fish," Dorothy Ann said. "A school!"

Ms. Frizzle leaned toward her mic. "That's right, D.A. And it looks like this school of fish has been practicing cool underwater moves."

"I can't believe you guys were all afraid of a bunch of dinky little fish," Ralphie laughed.

"Yeah, Ralphie, I forgot how brave you are. So, do you want to tackle that guy next?" said Keesha.

Everyone froze as a dark shadow swam up from the deep, dark bottom of the ocean.

"Ahhhhhhhhhh!" Ralphie screamed.

"SHARK!" they said together.

Dorothy Ann called information out in gasps. "Common name is blacktip reef shark of the family carcharhinidae and the genus—"

As quickly as the shark had appeared, it disappeared into the reef.

"Phew!" Carlos sighed. "I guess he had other fish to fry."

"That was close," Ralphie said. "Time for us to get outta here!"

"Class," Ms. Frizzle called out, "shake a tail fin."

The kids steered toward the bus—all except for Wanda. She was busy thinking about Becca.

"Wait, guys! We can't leave Becca. What about the shark? Guys? Guys!" Wanda called out to her classmates.

But they were already back inside the bus.

Wanda sighed and headed for the bus, too.

CHAPTER 5

DEEPWATER DIGS

Back on the beach, Wanda told her friends all about Becca Blue. And she explained why she was worried about her new fishy friend.

"That's an interesting question," Jyoti said. "How does something so small protect itself from something so huge?"

"Not just huge. **Enormous**, with big, sharp, pointy, scary, gnarr gnarr gnarr!" Wanda said, chomping her teeth.

"Look!" Carlos shouted. "A shark's tooth!"

"See how big it is?" Wanda said.

"According to my research," Dorothy Ann said, turning to her tablet, "sharks can have anywhere from five to fifty rows of teeth."

"Fifty rows of teeth?" asked Wanda, growing more and more worried about Becca Blue.

"Yes," replied Dorothy Ann. "Also, some fish hide in **coral reefs** to keep safe from predators. The reef acts kind of like a safe house with a tiny fish door."

CORAL REEF

A safe house? A fish door? Wanda smiled. *That's it!*

"Jyoti, I need one super-safe, super-high-tech fish house for Becca to hide in!" Wanda said. "You're so great at building things. Can you build it?"

"It might be tricky," Jyoti said. "I will need to build a saltwater-resistant house with cutting-edge technology."

"So, can you do it?" Wanda asked again.

Jyoti winked. "What color?"

Wanda smiled. Jyoti gathered tools, scrap materials, wire, electronics, hunks of coral, and seashells.

Soon, Jyoti was finished.

"Drum roll please," Jyoti said to Wanda. "Here is my super-high-tech underwater fish house with security system, alarms, and a video feed you can watch on your laptop."

Jyoti hadn't just built a fish *house*. She built a fish *mansion*!

"It's perfect!" Wanda exclaimed. "If that big, toothy shark gets anywhere near Becca, I'll know about it!"

Wanda swam out to sea and placed the house underwater. Becca zoomed inside.

"Hooray!" Wanda cheered. "She loves it—hey!"

Becca zoomed out just as fast as she had zoomed in.

"Where are you going?" Wanda asked.

Becca headed back out into the open sea.

Wanda's heart sank. *The shark is still out there,* she thought. *This is not good . . . Not good at all!*

CHAPTER 6
SINK OR SWIM

Wanda turned to her classmates.

"It's a great big ocean out there, and Becca is one tiny fish," Wanda said. "I'm not sure why she didn't stay inside the safe house we built. But we need to find her. I know she still needs our help. Who's with me?"

Wanda waited for a show of hands. But no one was paying attention to her. They were all watching Liz limbo on the beach.

"Becca needs our help," Wanda said again.

The other students grooved to a tropical beat as Liz slithered underneath the limbo bar.

"I'm sure Becca's fine, Wanda," Keesha said.

"Plus, she might go back to her new house," Jyoti pointed out.

"And the coral reef is there if she needs it," added Dorothy Ann.

"Grab a coconut soda, Wanda," Ralphie said. "It's time to have some fun!"

Arnold pointed to his beeping watch. "And it's time to reapply our sunscreen," he said.

Wanda tried to have fun. She cheered as Liz won the limbo contest by a tail! But she couldn't stop thinking about Becca.

"I'll just have to find Becca all by myself," Wanda said as she walked toward the sea. "Unless . . ."

Wanda walked over to her teacher. "Ms. Frizzle, can you help me find Becca Blue?"

Ms. Frizzle nodded. "Okay!" she said. "Let's see what we can do."

Wanda smiled.

"Liz, please keep an eye on the class," Ms. Frizzle called. "We've got a fish to find!"

Ms. Frizzle and Wanda hurried aboard the bus. It rolled straight to the **shoreline**, then dove deep down into the ocean.

Wanda looked out a window to search the water. There were so many fish in the sea. How would she ever find Becca?

Suddenly, Wanda spotted a tiny yellow-and-blue striped snapper darting around the underwater rocks. Becca Blue!

"There she is, Ms. Frizzle!" Wanda called.

Wanda climbed into her fishmobile.

"Don't worry, Becca!" she called. "Here I come!"

Wanda zoomed over to Becca. "I missed you, little scaly buddy!"

Becca hovered above the seaweed. Then she swam away again!

"Hey, wait up!" Wanda called.

Wanda chased after her friend. Just as she caught up, Becca darted off in a different direction.

Becca is a tough fish to follow, Wanda thought. *I never know where she is going to go next.*

Just then, a bright blue button on Wanda's control panel began to blink.

What's that? Wanda wondered. There was only one way to find out. She gave the button a tap and—

"Swimmer sense activated!" an electronic voice reported.

Swimmer-what? Wanda wondered.

A balloon lit up inside Wanda's fishmobile. Wanda held on tight as her fishmobile made a sharp drop. Then it rose up until it steadied itself in the water.

"Now at **optimum** swimming depth," the voice reported.

"Whoa!" Wanda exclaimed. "That balloon thingy must control how deep I am!"

Wanda saw a picture of her fishmobile on her monitor. Lines were lighting up on each side—from **gills** to tail!

"The lines on my fishmobile seem to be reacting to something in the water around me," Wanda said. "Only . . . why?"

"Friendly fish now approaching," said the electronic voice.

The fish was Becca. She was swimming right next to Wanda.

"Oh, that's why those lines lit up. Hi, Becca!" Wanda called.

The electronic voice spoke again, "Fishlink now engaged."

Wanda's fishmobile began to swim up and down with Becca. Wherever Becca went, Wanda went, too. They were completely in sync. Cool!

"Ms. Frizzle," Wanda called into her microphone, "I'm actually **synced** up to Becca. That line on Becca's side does that, too?"

"You got it, Wanda," Ms. Frizzle replied. "You're expert **synchronized** swimmers!"

Wanda was having so much fun that she almost missed the huge, dark shadow coming up from below.

"Uh-oh," said Wanda. "Maybe that's just another school of fish?"

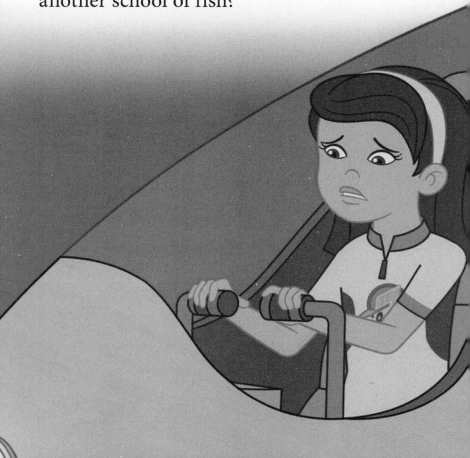

As the dark shape got closer, Wanda realized it could only be one thing. It wasn't hundreds of tiny fish swimming together. It was—

"The shark!" Wanda shouted.

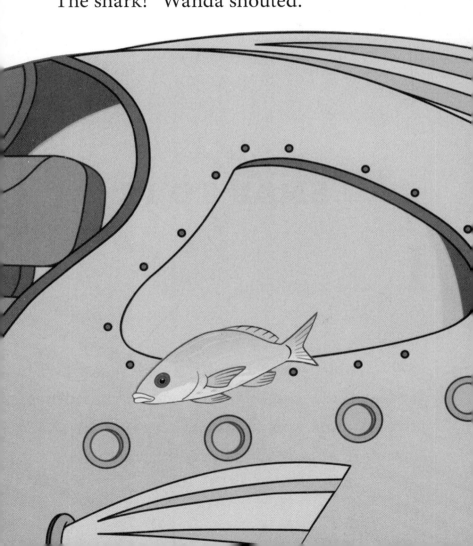

CHAPTER 7
SNAP TO IT

Is there a problem, Wanda?" Ms. Frizzle's voice asked over the microphone. "Are you in trouble?"

"Nothing I can't handle," said Wanda. "I'll distract the shark to turn it away from Becca. Then I'll hide while Becca escapes."

"Okay," said Ms. Frizzle. "Be careful!"

Wanda yanked the joystick, pushing the fishmobile forward. Becca swam forward, too, in the same direction as Wanda.

"No, Becca," Wanda said. "You go the other way." But Becca kept following Wanda's fishmobile. "Becca, swim!"

Suddenly, Wanda realized the problem. The fishlink was still on! She pushed the blinking button again, and the depth meter on her fishmobile went dark. The line faded from its side.

"Fishlink disengaged," the electronic voice reported.

"Now go, Becca, go!" shouted Wanda.

While Becca swam off, Wanda headed for a hiding place under some rocks. She expected the shark to follow her, but instead it followed Becca!

"Oh, no!" Wanda groaned.

Just then, an enormous group of blue-and-yellow stripers appeared. They looked just like Becca.

"Those must be her school friends," Wanda said. "All together they look like one huge creature!"

The giant shimmering ball of fish split in two. The shark was confused. It swam after one half of the group first. Then it tried to chase the other.

"Nice one." Wanda laughed. "Now he doesn't know what to chase!"

The shark dove toward the middle of one of the schools. Hundreds of fish shot off in different directions.

"Find your lunch somewhere else!" shouted Wanda.

But the shark tried again. This time it was headed directly for Wanda!

CHAPTER 8
SHARK BAIT

Ms. Frizzle decided Wanda needed some help! She called the class on her tablet.

"Okay, class, listen up," Ms. Frizzle told them. "It's time to go to school."

"School?" asked Ralphie. "I thought we were not saying the *S* word today!"

An image flashed on Dorothy Ann's screen. The shark was closing in on Wanda's fishmobile!

Keesha didn't waste one second. She raced toward the ocean. "We have to help Wanda!" she shouted. "Come on, everybody!"

"Is that the shark?" Carlos said. "Cool!"

"But Wanda's about to be shark chow!" Jyoti said.

"Less cool," Carlos sighed.

"We should not have stayed home today," said Arnold to Liz as he ran toward the bus. "Wanda needs our help."

"Time for Operation Save Wanda—the way the locals do it!" said Ms. Frizzle. The bus turned into a submarine and carried the class under the sea.

The bus spit out the class's fishmobiles. But Wanda was nowhere to be found. Everyone looked and looked.

Suddenly, Carlos spied a fishmobile poking out from behind a rock.

"Wanda!" he called.

Wanda spotted Carlos, too. He was nearby in his fishmobile, and he was not alone. Keesha, Tim, Jyoti, Dorothy Ann, Ralphie, and Arnold were there, too!

"Are you okay, Wanda?" Keesha asked.

"I thought you were all too busy to help Becca," Wanda said.

"But we care about you," Tim said.

"We're here for you, Wanda," Dorothy Ann said. "You need help, don't you?"

"Well, yes. So much!" Wanda admitted. "Did you guys see the shark? I can't get away from this rock without going snout-to-snout with old gnarr-gnarr face."

"You need some fish-style help," Tim told Wanda. "From your own school—us!"

CHAPTER 9

BETTER TOGETHER

Stay here," Keesha said to Wanda. "We'll try to distract the shark."

Keesha drove her fishmobile past the shark. The shark turned to follow Keesha, and Wanda knew it was her only chance.

Here goes nothing, Wanda thought.

She moved out from behind the rock and made a swim for it! The shark was too fast. He headed for Wanda, but found Arnold instead.

"Yipes! Don't eat *me*!" Arnold yelled from his fishmobile. "I taste like SPF 100! You won't like it!"

Arnold yanked his joystick. His fishmobile flipped upside down. Then it shot backward out of the shark's way.

The shark looked around for someone new—Dorothy Ann!

"Uh-oh." She gulped. "According to my research, I'm toast!"

Wanda zoomed by in her fishmobile. "Hey, look over here, shark!" she shouted.

The shark ditched Dorothy Ann to chase Wanda. Then it went after Carlos.

"We can't do this all day!" said Carlos.

Ms. Frizzle shouted, "As my rock-and-roll relative, Great Auntie Palooza, used to say, maybe it's time to get your acts together!"

Together! Wanda thought. *That's it!*

Wanda smiled at the magic word. She leaned toward her mic and began to shout, "Fishlink! Fishlink!"

"What? Did you sneeze?" Ralphie asked.

Wanda waved her arm wildly over the control panel. "No! Hit the fishlink button NOW! It's the blinking blue button right in front of you!" she exclaimed.

Wanda pressed the blue button. The depth meter lit up and the lines at the sides of her fishmobile flashed.

"Got it," said Jyoti, pushing the button.

"Fishlink now engaged," the electronic voice reported.

The lines on the sides of Jyoti's fishmobile lit up as she fell into perfect synchronization with Wanda.

The rest of the class hit their blue buttons.

"Follow me, everyone!" Wanda declared.

The school of fishmobiles moved through the water. They moved up, they moved down, and they moved side to side—together.

"It's like we all share one great big giant fish brain!" Carlos pointed out.

Keesha laughed. "That would be gross, if it weren't so *awesome.*"

The class was outsmarting the shark with every move.

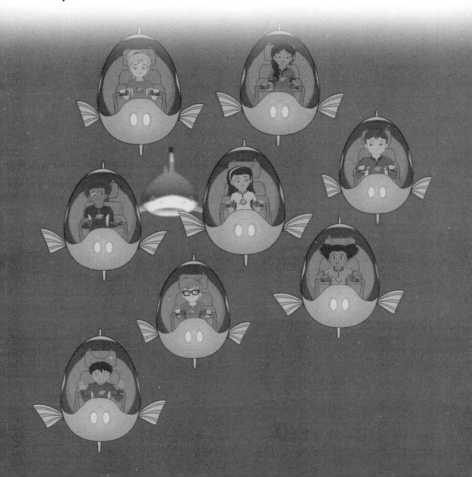

"As my older sister might say," Ms. Frizzle exclaimed, "woo-hooooo!"

But they weren't safe yet. They might have fooled the shark for a minute, but he was smart. They had to get out of there—fast!

"Let's show this guy what scary is all about!" Wanda said. "Remember how we got scared by the giant blob? When all those little fish looked like one big fish?"

"Totally!" they all shouted.

"It's blob-building time!" Wanda said.

The students began to form one giant blob of fishmobiles. Together they were even bigger than the shark!

The school of fishmobiles headed straight for the shark. The giant blob looked so big and powerful that the shark didn't know what to do!

He turned the other way, but the school chased him.

"You're not getting away that easy," said Carlos.

Finally, the shark disappeared into the deep, dark sea.

"See ya later!" said Wanda.

"We scared the shark! We did it!" Keesha cheered.

"Together," Wanda added.

The fishmobiles headed toward the bus.

"Students, it's time for another school: our own!" called Ms. Frizzle. "Bus, do your stuff!"

CHAPTER 10

ALOHA, WALKERVILLE

Ms. Frizzle's students said "Aloha" to sunny Hawaii and "Aloha" to a cold, snowy Walkerville. In Hawaii, Aloha means hello *and* goodbye!

Ms. Frizzle sang in Hawaiian as she hung a Hawaii poster in the classroom.

"Huh?" Arnold said. "What does that mean?"

"School's out for the rest of our lives?" joked Ralphie.

"No, Ralphie. I was just singing in Hawaiian that today's field trip was incredible," Ms. Frizzle explained.

"It was pretty amazing," Tim agreed.

"Bustin' out those slick fish moves and schooling that shark!" Carlos said.

"I can't believe I went to all that trouble to save Becca when she already had all the help she needed," Wanda said.

"That is one fish with some pretty great friends," Jyoti said.

Wanda smiled at her classmates. "Yeah," she said. "I know the feeling!"

Arnold sighed. "I just wish I knew why we had to come back from Hawaii so soon."

"Well, I do try to wrap up field trips before three o'clock," said Ms. Frizzle.

"Just this once," Arnold pleaded, "I wish that trip had lasted until summer o'clock!"

The class laughed.

Then they looked out the window at the freezing piles of snow and ice.

"Well, since nobody wants to go outside in the cold," said Wanda, grabbing her giant scrapbook, "who wants to hear about the poor Aleutian shield fern? I could go on for hours—"

But the classroom door slammed before Wanda finished her sentence. Everyone—even Arnold—had decided to brave the outdoors.

"Look at them playing together," said Ms. Frizzle as she looked out the window. "Remind you of anything, Wanda?"

Wanda pressed a pretend button.

"BOOP!" she joked, heading for the door. "Yep, kidlink now engaged."

GLOSSARY

Activate: to turn on or cause to work

Coral reef: an underwater chain of rocks, tiny skeletons, and other materials

Enormous: extremely big

Family: a group of plants or animals that are related to one another

Genus: a group of related plants or animals that is larger than a species but smaller than a family

Gills: a pair of organs near a fish's mouth through which it breathes

Optimum: the best or most favorable

Shoreline: where a body of water meets the land

State-of-the-art: the newest or most up to date

Sync (short for *synchronize*): two events happening together at the same time

Ukulele: a small, four-stringed guitar originally made popular in Hawaii

Ask Professor Frizzle

Are all fish good swimmers?

Yes! Besides using their fins to swim, they can twist their bodies so they can push the water. They are the gymnasts of the deep!

I know fish school for protection, but I have an aquarium full of schooling fish and they have nothing to be afraid of. What's up with that?

That's because there are lots of reasons to school besides protection. Sometimes fish school for feeding and sweep through the water like a giant net, munching on their favorite seafood as they go.

The buttons that control the fish sense in the fishmobiles were cool, but real fish don't have buttons. Do they?

 Good observation. Real fish have a sack of gas inside them called a swim bladder, which tells them how deep they are, and controls whether and how much they sink or float.

What is the purpose of lines on their sides?

 Stylish and functional. The lateral lines on the side of their bodies sense tiny changes in the water, telling them when other fish or tasty bits are nearby.

Why are sharks always the bad guys? Is this really true in real life?

 It's so not fair! Sharks may be dangerous, but they're just trying to survive! Plus, you'll be glad to know they almost never hurt people.

Thanks for all of your help, Professor Frizzle!

 You're very welcome. This went swimmingly! 🐟

The Magic School Bus Rides Again

QUESTIONS and ACTIVITIES

1. Ms. Frizzle's class escaped the snowy weather to go on a tropical adventure! If you could go on a trip, where in the world would you go?

2. Jyoti made a fish mansion for Wanda's fishy friend, Becca! Draw your own underwater house.

3. How do you think Wanda feels when her classmates show up to help her escape the shark?

4. A shark was out to get the class! How does the class outsmart the shark?

5. At the end of the story, Wanda jokes, "Kidlink now engaged." What do you think she means by that?